LEGO CITY
5-MINUTE STORIES

Random House 🏠 New York

Illustrated by
AMEET Studio

LEGO, the LEGO logo, the Minifigure and the Brick and Knob configurations are trademarks and/or copyrights of the LEGO Group. All rights reserved.
©2023 The LEGO Group.

 Manufactured under license granted to AMEET Sp. z o.o. by the LEGO Group.

AMEET Sp. z o.o.
Nowe Sady 6, 94–102 Łódź—Poland
ameet@ameet.eu
www.ameet.eu

www.LEGO.com

Published in the United States by Random House Children's Books, a division of Penguin Random House LLC, 1745 Broadway, New York, NY 10019, and in Canada by Penguin Random House Canada Limited, Toronto. Random House and the colophon are registered trademarks of Penguin Random House LLC.

rhcbooks.com

Educators and librarians, for a variety of teaching tools, visit us at RHTeachersLibrarians.com

ISBN 978-0-593-43155-9 (trade) — ISBN 978-0-593-43156-6 (ebook)

MANUFACTURED IN CHINA

10 9 8 7 6 5 4 3 2 1

CONTENTS

BEST BIRTHDAY EVER

Based on the story by Stacia Deutsch

"**H**appy birthday to me!" Harl Hubbs sang as he bounced out of bed. "It's my special day!" He hurried outside and exclaimed, "To celebrate my birthday, I am going to help as many citizens as possible!" Humming the "Happy Birthday" song to himself, Harl rushed down the street, eager to start the day.

The first person he saw was Lieutenant Duke DeTain, outside the police station.

"Yee-ha!" Duke shouted as he executed a perfect shoulder roll that ended with a crouching jump-kick. "Hello, Helpful Handyman!" He winked at Harl. "You weren't planning on making any trouble, were ya?" He wiggled his eyebrows.

"Nope, never any trouble from me," Harl said with a laugh. "Today's my birthday. I'm planning to have a happy helpy day."

"That sounds perfectly Harl-ly, " said Duke.

"Need anything?" Harl asked, pointing at his toolbox.

Duke considered Harl's offer. "Well, I was looking for something exciting to do today," he said. "Seems the crooks are all taking the day off. If you think of anything fun for me to do, you know where I'll be!" Then he tucked and rolled toward the station house.

"I'm on it," Harl said. "One extra-exciting day coming right up!"

Harl found Firefighter Bob reading a magazine outside the fire station.

"Got any helping handy things I can do?" Harl greeted.

"Nope," Bob said with a yawn. "It's a quiet day."

Harl had an idea. "Last time you were racing out to action, I noticed the truck siren sounded a little quiet. I'm here to help," he said, holding up a screwdriver. Before Bob could reply, Harl was on the job. He rewired the siren. "All done," Harl announced proudly.

Bob pressed the button. *Bock-bock!* The siren clucked like a chicken.

"Hmm. That's not right!" Harl said, scratching his head. "Let me try again—" He raised his screwdriver, and suddenly a whirring alarm echoed through the firehouse.

"My truck's been Harled!" Firefighter Bob said, straightening his helmet. "Gotta go! Our best cluck-truck to the rescue!" He jumped into the fire truck and clicked on the squawking siren. People on the street turned to stare. "I must admit, it is louder . . . ," Bob remarked as he sped away.

Harl watched the fire engine race off. He felt bad for a moment that his fix hadn't gone as planned. But then he puffed out his chest and announced, "It's still my special day. I'll turn this frown upside down by helping someone else."

Harl rode his bicycle through City Center Square and noticed that Poppy Starr's music performance stage was in pieces. He said to himself, 'Looks like she could use a hand!' Poppy was busy taking selfies with her fans. Harl didn't want to bother her, so he got to work, swinging his hammer wildly, putting the stage together.

Minutes later, Poppy found Harl checking the sound equipment. "You're ready for a show!" he declared.

"Uh, Harl?" Poppy said as he handed her a microphone. "I was taking the stage down, not building it up."

"Oh," Harl said with a grimace. "That's unfortunate."

Poppy shrugged. "No worries. I gotta run to a big meeting about my next hit song." Then she dashed away.

Harl sighed sadly.

Harl was still in the city square when Shirley Keeper came by. She was carrying an empty trash can.

"What's up?" Shirley asked Harl.

"I'm having a rough day," Harl admitted.

Shirley grunted. "Me too. Not much trash to collect today."

"How about I give the truck a tune-up, then?" Harl suggested as he dug out parts from his toolbox. "I've been itching to install a laser nuclear extreme-voltage trash-detection system!"

"No thanks, Harl," Shirley said as she put the can on the curb. "It's quitting time." She swung up into her truck. "Want to ride with me tomorrow? You could pass out copies of the City Waste-Management Guidelines. People need to read the rules!"

"I suppose . . . ," Harl said with a groan as Shirley drove away. He sat on the pavement and muttered, "But tomorrow won't be my special day anymore."

Suddenly, Duke DeTain appeared next to Harl. "Find me something fun to do yet?" he asked.

"No. Nothing's going on today," Harl moaned. "It's the worst birthday ever."

Duke wrinkled his brow. "You seem sad," he said.

"Yes, I am," Harl said as he put his head in his hands.

Duke jumped up and announced, "The day's not over yet!" He disappeared as quickly as he'd appeared.

Harl went home. The day was nearly over, and he hadn't helped even one person.

Suddenly, someone knocked on Harl's door. It was Fire Chief Freya McCloud. She showed him a tangle of string lights and asked, "Can you unwind these?"

Harl felt his spirits lift. "Happy to help," he said.

After the chief left, Mayor Fleck arrived. "I've been looking all over for you. Can you get my groceries at the store?" he asked. "I'm so busy! Don't ask me what I'm doing, but it's very important."

"I'm happy to help," Harl said with a smile. Then he went to get his bike.

While Harl was delivering the groceries to the mayor's office, Police Chief Wheeler stopped him. "Hey, handy-dude!" the chief exclaimed. He was carrying his skateboard. "My front wheel's busted. Unless you fix it, I can't do anything awesome or gnarly."

"Happy to help!" Harl said, grinning. "But I need to take the groceries first. . . ."

"Wheeler never walks!" the chief exclaimed as he took the groceries and shoved his board into Harl's hands. "I have spare wheels in my office. Let's go!"

"B-b-b-but—" Harl stammered. "I suppose the mayor can wait. I'M HAPPY TO HELP!"

Harl went with Chief Wheeler into the police station. "I'll need a 9/16 Allen wrench—" Harl began.

"SURPRISE!" Harl's friends shouted as they jumped out from behind desks and chairs. The mayor revealed that the box of groceries contained a big cake. Chief McCloud flicked a switch and the twinkle lights that Harl had unwound glittered like stars.

"Happy birthday, Harl!" everyone shouted.

"Thanks for helping me today!" Firefighter Bob said.

"I didn't help," Harl told him. "I made the fire engine siren cluck."

"It was exactly what we needed when we went to find the lost baby chicks. They followed the fire truck like it was their mama," said Bob, shaking Harl's hand. "All the chicks are safe, thanks to you."

Poppy said, "The recording studio wants a concert tonight! I'm gonna need to stand on that stage you built while I sing for my adoring fans. Thanks for your help, Harl! I'll get you a ticket!"

"Wow!" Harl said, blushing. Then he asked Shirley Keeper, "Any chance I helped you, too, and didn't know it?"

"No, I'm afraid not . . . yet!" she said, pointing at the empty trash can. "But you will. I see a lot of trash coming soon. This party's gonna get messy!"

19

Duke put his arm around Harl and said, "You helped a lot of people today."

Harl told Duke, "I never found something exciting for you to do."

"Fighting crime is the tops," Duke said. "But planning your top-secret surprise party was fun, and entertaining as well!" He gave a hearty thumbs-up and a big grin.

"I'm glad I could help!" Harl cheered, looking around at his friends. "This is the best birthday ever!"

COSTUME CAPERS

BEEP! BEEP! BEEP!

Based on the story by Kelly McKain

Mayor Fleck's alarm clock went off, and he sat up in bed. "It's Monday," he said, "which is a workday. I love work."

He eagerly got out of bed and went to the bathroom. "Hmm . . . that's odd," he said. Something felt strange, but he couldn't figure out what it was. While he took a shower, he figured it out. *"ARGH!"* he cried. "My corn outfit! I never take it off! Where has it gone?"

He searched his apartment, but he couldn't find the corn outfit anywhere. In a panic, he put on a simple suit from his closet and rushed to work.

Mayor Fleck arrived at Town Hall. His
assistant, Carol Yea, stopped him before
he entered his office.

"Excuse me, sir, the mayor isn't here
yet," she said. "Is he expecting you?"

"I am the mayor," Mayor Fleck insisted.
"Don't you recognize me?"

"Um . . . n-no . . . ," Carol stammered.

The mayor looked at Carol's daughter, Madison, who had come to work with her mom. The mayor asked her, "You know me, don't you, Small Carol?"

"Mommy, who is this stranger?" whispered Madison.

"You seem a little confused, sir," said Carol. "Please take a seat. The mayor will be here soon."

Mayor Fleck took a seat and waited for himself to arrive. "Wait a minute. I AM the mayor!" he cried. "It's ME! Can't you see?"

Carol frowned and looked closer and closer, until . . . She gasped. "*ARGH!* It *is* you! But, sir, you don't look like you!"

"I really don't feel like myself, either!" said the mayor.

Carol became worried. "Even with my boundless optimism, I can see that this is not a good situation," she said.

Mayor Fleck quickly found out what she meant. Without his corn outfit, no one recognized him all morning.

He tried to sign off on a new construction site, but no one wanted to start working until the "real mayor" showed up.

He tried to open a new shopping center, but no one believed he was the mayor. The new shops stayed closed, and no one could work!

He went to visit the new wing of the hospital, but everyone thought he was a confused patient who'd bumped his head.

Back at the mayor's office, Carol was worried. "Unless people recognize you, you can't do any work." She frowned. "The city will fall apart!"

"ARGH!" cried Mayor Fleck. "Not do any work?" He couldn't even imagine that.

Suddenly, Madison had an idea. "I know!" she cried, and rushed out.

Before they knew it, she was back—with her friend Billy and an airplane costume.

"If you wear a costume, everyone will know who you are," Madison explained.

"Hmm . . . I don't know, but I'll give it a try," said Mayor Fleck. He put on the costume . . . and smiled. "This outfit is excellent. Thank you!"

Unfortunately, the costume's wings were so long that Mayor Fleck couldn't turn or move!

"Look! There's a button on this airplane," said Billy. "Maybe the wings will fold down if we press it."

But when Billy pressed the button, the wings didn't fold. Instead, the propeller started to spin, and . . . the mayor flew into the air! *Whoosh!*

"Heeeeelp!" cried Mayor Fleck as he shot across the room and right out the window.

CRASH! Luckily, instead of hitting the ground, Mayor Fleck landed right on top of Harl the Handyman's bicycle.

"Thanks for breaking my fall," the mayor said, freeing himself from the airplane costume.

"Happy to help, flying stranger!" said Harl.

"Believe it or not, it's Mayor Fleck!" Madison called from the window. "He needs a new special outfit, and soon!"

"No problem!" cried Harl, a little surprised. "I've just been to my ballet class, Mayor, so you can borrow my tutu!"

Back in his office, Mayor Fleck put on the tutu and did a twirl. "I like it," he told them. "I think it will help my image. Nothing says 'work' like a pink sparkly tutu."

He picked up his pen, which for some reason had turned into a banana. Then he tried to sit down at his desk to work, but . . . the skirt bunched up around his face.

Mayor Fleck frowned. "Oh, no—I can't see! This skirt stops me from doing my work."

"Quick, we need a different costume!" cried Carol. She picked up the telephone . . . which, surprisingly, had turned into a banana. "I'll call Freya. She always has good ideas in a pinch!"

It wasn't long before a fire truck screeched up in front of Town Hall and Freya dashed up the ladder. "Here you go!" she said, handing over a blue bundle. "Try this!"

Soon the mayor had squeezed into the new costume. Now he was dressed as a ninja and was holding nunchucks.

"What are these?" he asked, swinging them around.

"Um, sir, they're actually . . . ," began Freya. But it was too late. The nunchucks slipped out of the mayor's hands and flew across the office. Everyone ducked as the nunchucks swung past their heads and knocked over a vase and a lamp.

"Hmm, all this smashing is distracting me from my work," said Mayor Fleck. "I need a new costume, right away—before the city falls apart!"

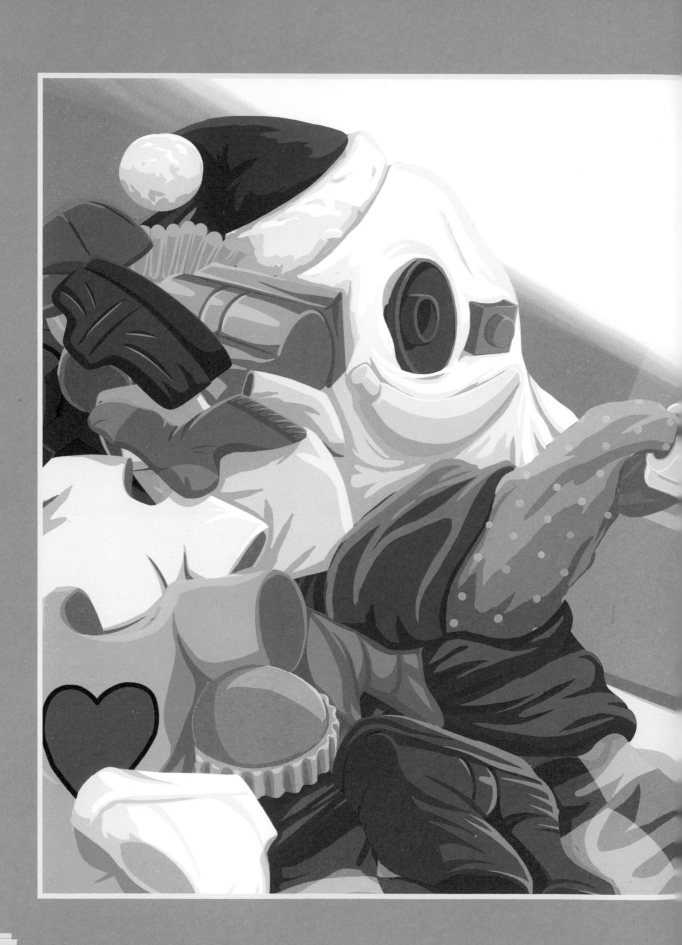

This time, Madison and her friends came back with a huge crowd and lots of fun outfits.

The mayor was a majorette and then a cloud and then a washing machine. His head started to spin. "No, no, no," he said.

Then he was a book and a bee and a cupcake. His brain started to boggle. "No, no, no!" he cried, backing away from the crowd. "Stop this! No more!"

No one listened. Next he was a walrus and then a pixie and then even a slice of cheese. There was a whole avalanche of costumes!

"Help!" wailed the mayor. "It's a nightmare!"

BEEP! BEEP! BEEP!

What was that?

It sounded exactly like his alarm clock.

He sat up in his bed.

The mayor gasped. "Oh, I was dreaming! It actually *was* a nightmare! Well, I suppose that makes sense. And in the nightmare I was wearing a bunch of colorful costumes. That would never happen in real life."

Mayor Fleck got out of bed and looked down at himself. Phew! He was wearing his beloved, completely sensible corn outfit, just like he did on every other ordinary day.

"It's so good that everything's back to normal!" said the mayor. "And fortunately, things won't turn into bananas anymore. . . ."

THE PERFECT TRICK

Based on the story by Matt Killeen

It was a typical day at police headquarters, which meant that Sergeant Sam Grizzled and Detective Rooky Partnur had just closed another case. Rooky was opening her mail when she got a pleasant surprise.

"Wow!" Rooky shouted suddenly. "I got tickets for the Stunt Show!"

"Sounds like it will be noisy," Sam growled.

"Come with me to the show," Rooky pleaded. "You'll love it. I used to skateboard as a kid. I watched stunts all the time. We can talk about work there."

"Not my thing," Sam replied firmly. "Too busy," he added, sighing.

Rooky looked at Sam's desk. "I'll do your paperwork for y—"

"What time shall I meet you?" Sam said quickly.

Soon they were at the show.

"Ready to meet the crew?" yelled Doug Dynamo, the announcer.

The crowd cheered and waved. The stadium went dark except for one pool of light.

"Great. Now I can't see my hot dog," moaned Sam.

The announcer continued. "First up—he turns science even more AWESOME. It's . . . Rocket Racer!"

"My favorite!" cried Rooky as the crowd roared.

The motorcyclist burst into the arena, a blur of color under the lights.
Rocket Racer waved to the audience and accelerated toward a ramp. The barrels beyond it caught fire. The stadium screamed!

Up and over he flipped, arms in the air, before landing on his back wheel. The crowd went wild.

"Did you see that, Grizzled?" Rooky yelled, slapping Sam's arm.

"Yep, I'm sitting right here," Sam grumbled.

The mind-blowing stunts went on. Monster trucks leapt over cars. There were explosions and mechanical spiders. When Rooky wasn't jumping up and down, she watched the whole thing open-mouthed.

"This is just . . . awesome," she breathed.

Sam was having trouble staying awake.

"What use is this in the real world?" he moaned.

Rooky didn't hear him. Watching Rocket flying off a ramp, she suddenly thought back to when she was a kid, hopping on a shiny new skateboard . . . and soaring through the air!

The next morning, Rooky burst into the police station. "I found it!" she shouted, happily holding a dusty skateboard. "I don't know why I ever stopped riding it."

"Because it has a unicorn on it?" Sam said, looking up briefly.

"I was eight. Anyway, unicorns are awesome!" Rooky exclaimed. "Want to go to the skate park at lunchtime?"

"Do they sell donuts?" asked Sam.

"There's a donut shop next door," Rooky replied.

"Then I'm in," Sam agreed.

The sergeant wasn't happy about being dragged to the skate park, but he did get his donuts. Rooky was talking to two skaters named Maddy and Billy.

Despite her enthusiasm, Rooky found skateboarding very difficult. She didn't remember anything she had learned as a girl. She moved from trick to trick, but they were all really hard.

"Um, maybe you should try one trick to start?" Maddy suggested gently.

"No time! I need to work on everything," Rooky said, jumping on her board. "Let's go!"

Bored as he was, Sam noticed that Rooky was getting bumps and bruises.

"Hey, Detective. Hey . . . ," Sam called as Maddy and Billy helped her up again. "Rooky, I think you need to stop."

"It's fun," Rooky wailed. But everything was hurting. "I'm just a bit tired."

"Doesn't *look* fun," said Sam.

"But I can't quit!" she howled. "I need one perfect trick."

"You know what the problem is?" asked a voice.
Everyone turned to see . . . Rocket Racer!
Rooky gasped. "What are *you* doing here?" she
said. "Sorry, hello!"
"Hi! I like to take my skateboard out on tour,"
Rocket explained. "You're working hard, Detective,
but not working smart. . . ."

Rocket sat Rooky down. He told her that she was trying tricks that were too advanced. She needed to master the basics first.

She had to practice the push, stop, and turn, and then learn one trick at a time.

"Once you've 'made' your trick, keep at it," he said.

So, with Rocket's help, Rooky chose one trick and put all her effort into it.

After getting it right, she did it again. And again. Until it was perfect!

Suddenly, Sam and Rooky got a call from dispatch on their radio.

"All units. Robbery at donut shop . . ."

"That's next door!" Rooky said.

"Fugitive heading south—" the radio continued.

"And coming right to us!" Rooky shouted.

Just then, the crook, Hacksaw Hank, leapt over the wall with a huge bag of cash. He spotted Sam and Rooky and ran for the gate.

"Stop, in the name of the law!" shouted Rooky.

Before the sergeant got up from his bench, Rooky was pushing off after the robber on her skateboard. The crook had a head start, but she knew she could catch up. . . .

Push!

Hank darted into the street with Rooky hot on his heels. He weaved through a traffic jam.

Turn!

She kicked the skateboard into a series of fast turns, cutting the distance between them. Looking back, Hank yelped.

Rooky leaned right, carving into some
roadwork and toward a large piece of
wood leaning on a pile of sand.

She hit the ramp and soared into the
air. Catching her skateboard, Rooky sailed
over Hank's head. She landed cleanly and
stopped right in front of him, dropping
handcuffs onto his wrists. The perfect trick!

"Wow! I'd applaud, but I can't move my hands," said Hank.

Back at the skate park, Rooky thanked Rocket, Maddy, and Billy for their help and advice. It had definitely paid off.

Sam looked sheepish.

"I was . . . wrong," he mumbled. "Doing something you love and doing it well makes you a better person . . . and a better cop."

"Gee, thanks, Grizzled!" Rooky smiled, blushing. "Hey, we've got eight minutes of lunch left. Think I can nail the kickflip?"

TRAINING DAY

Based on the story by Karolina Kitala

It was early in the morning, but the hardworking firefighters had been up for hours, already busy with their duties for the day. In fact, Feldman, Clemmons, and Bob were so busy, they didn't even notice Fire Chief Freya McCloud approaching.

"I have a surprise for you," the chief announced
excitedly as she walked into the firehouse. "We're
going to test out some brand-new equipment today!
Are you ready for an exciting training session?"

"You bet!" cried the firefighters. They cheerfully
followed their chief out to the training grounds.

Chief McCloud started the training by showing everyone a new obstacle-removal vehicle.

"At a fire, this large bulldozer will help us get into hard-to-reach places and move anything that gets in our way," she said with a smile.

"What a great machine! I sure would love to drive it," said Feldman.

"The first firefighter to test the bulldozer will be . . . Bob," said the chief.

Feldman was a little disappointed but did not complain. Bob eagerly got into the vehicle and started the engine. He was all smiles as he prepared to take the new vehicle for a test drive. He was sure he'd do well.

However, things did not go according to plan. Bob wanted to back up, but somehow he made the bulldozer drive forward instead. Before he could figure out what he had done wrong, the powerful machine crashed through a rack full of fire extinguishers and sent them flying in every direction. *WHAM!*

Bob was unable to control the bulldozer. It turned and drove right toward his fellow firefighters. Clemmons and Feldman dove out of the way just in time, but they landed with a *THUD* on Roastie, the intelligent firefighting robot!

A bit rattled, Bob climbed down from the bulldozer. "I'm sorry . . . ," he muttered sadly.

The fire chief winced as the other firefighters untangled themselves and slowly got back on their feet. Everyone was okay, but the bulldozer test was a failure!

"Well, never mind that," said Chief McCloud. "Let's move on to the next piece of equipment. This new fire hose can handle twice as much water as our old one! That's double the firefighting power!"

"Awesome! We'll put out fires even faster and be able to get back to the station for dessert," Bob said happily. "I can't wait to give this baby a try!"

But the chief asked Clemmons to test the new hose. The skittish firefighter was afraid of everything—even spicy pizza! Even a picture of spicy pizza! With his face full of panic and his whole body shaking, he approached the new equipment and prepared to test it out.

Chief McCloud turned on the valve, and water immediately gushed all over. Clemmons, gripping the hose, whirled through the air, the hose blasting water on everything. He couldn't control it!

"AAHH!" shouted Clemmons.

SPLOOOSH! Water sprayed the equipment and the firefighters.

The chief turned off the valve as quickly as she could. Clemmons immediately fell from midair and landed in a puddle on the ground with a *SPLAT!*

"I just . . . I only . . . ," the shaken, soggy firefighter whispered while the other firefighters happily splashed around in the new puddles.

"Well, accidents happen . . . and they're sure happening a lot today," the chief said with a sigh as she unloaded a new piece of equipment off the back of the truck. "Anyway, last but not least, we have this modern fire rover."

"Whoa! Cool water cannon!" Clemmons said.

"Chief, can I test it?" Feldman asked.

"Sure," said the chief, and handed her the rover's remote control. "Just be careful!"

CLICK! CLICK! CLICK! Feldman pressed some buttons, finally activating the rover—but she couldn't figure out how to control it. And when she pressed a green button, instead of ordinary water, the rover shot out a powerful icy stream!

ZAP! The stream hit Roastie . . . and froze him solid!

"Sorry! I don't know how that happened!" said Feldman.

The firefighters immediately started freeing Roastie.

The chief was not pleased. She looked around in disbelief. The training was a total disaster. "I think we have to cancel the—"

Just then, the alarm sounded! The firefighters jumped
to their feet and ran quickly to the fire station to get
ready. The skyscraper construction site was on fire!

It was time for action. Bob, Clemmons, and Feldman
grabbed their equipment, jumped into the fire engine,
and headed out. Fire Chief McCloud was right beside
them in the new bulldozer.

The firefighters raced to the scene with the equipment
they had tested earlier. This time, the chief decided that
Feldman would control the bulldozer, Bob would handle

the new hose, and Clemmons would command the rover. Swapping duties was a terrific decision!

Feldman often rode Roastie, so she was a natural at operating the bulldozer. She removed obstacles for the entire team.

Thanks to Bob's training at the gym, he was fantastic at keeping control of the powerful fire hose.

Clemmons easily handled the rover cannon—he felt like he was playing his favorite video game!

They put the fire out in no time.

"I'm very proud of you, team!" said the chief, and they toasted with steaming cups of hot cocoa. "You've all passed the training today!"

"But how?" asked Clemmons.

"Yeah," said Feldman. "We all messed up!"

"With every single piece of equipment," Bob added.

The fire chief smiled. "We discovered the most important thing—what everyone is best at doing! And even more important than that, we put out the fire—as a team."

DUKE ON THE CHASE

Based on the story by Karolina Kitala

It was another beautiful, sunny day in the city. Police officer Duke DeTain had been patrolling the streets since early in the morning. Super-fast chases and catching crooks were his specialties— but things had been quiet so far. That changed when he suddenly got an urgent message about a bank robbery!

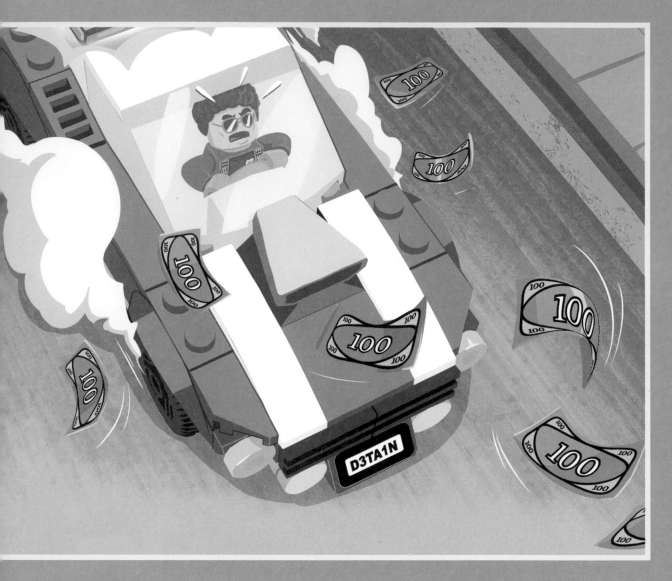

Duke's smart police car reported, "Several bags of money have been stolen from the bank, and Daisy Kaboom was spotted at the scene of the crime. She was last seen speeding away in a bright red truck!"

Duke hit the accelerator. *VROOM!* "We have to catch her as fast as we can!" Duke said to his car. "Luckily, if there's two things I'm good at, it's catching bad guys and going fast!"

But as Duke sped down the street, he noticed it was raining . . . cash!

"According to my latest data, that is the money from the robbery," said the police car.

"And according to MY data," Duke said, "Daisy's making a big mess!"

"If we follow the money, it should lead us to her," said the car.

"And when we find her, we'll write her a ticket for littering," Duke said as they quickly followed the trail.

The money led Duke straight to Daisy, who was speeding through town and had taken a dangerous shortcut through the city parking lot.

People on the sidewalk stopped and stared. They had never seen a police car racing after a truck leaving a trail of floating money!

"You'll never catch me!" Daisy yelled as Duke's police car closed in. "But it doesn't hurt to make sure," she added to herself as she sped up and pulled out a bundle of dynamite. She lit the fuse and tossed the explosives toward a parked truck carrying a load of logs!

BOOM! CRASH! BAM!

Logs flew through the air!

"Tim-BER!" Daisy yelled, laughing as she sped away from Duke and the tumbling logs.

But Duke wasn't discouraged. His car's super sensors detected the hazard, and the officer skillfully dodged the logs as they bounced toward him.

"I liked it better when it was just raining money!" he said, steering around the last of the falling logs.

"Ugh!" yelled Daisy. "What a waste of time . . . and dynamite!" Her trick hadn't worked!

"Remember to write Daisy a ticket for unauthorized use of explosives," Duke said to his car.

The chase continued as Duke pursued Daisy at top speed, while money continued to fly out of the back of the speeding truck.

The officer pursued Daisy as fast as he could, but she had no plans to be arrested.

"Sorry, Duke!" the crook cried as she zipped around a tight curve. "You'll never catch me!"

Hopping a curb, Daisy veered off the road and into a construction zone. She zoomed around the huge machinery, but Duke was right on her tail. Daisy just missed hitting a truck carrying bricks! And she was nearly cut off by Duke and his car. The officer was closing in fast.

"You're trapped now, Daisy. There's nowhere to go," said Duke.

"Ha! Don't be so sure!" Daisy replied. "I think YOU'RE the one going down!" She made a sharp turn. *SCREEEECH!*

Driving at top speed, the police officer wondered aloud, "Why would she turn . . . ?"

Duke soon discovered why—he saw a big open manhole right in front of him.

Uh-oh! With no time to slow down, the car was going to fall down into the sewer!

Duke thought fast. Just before his car plunged into the yucky water, he managed to throw a magnetic

transmitter toward Daisy's car. *ZZZZZIP!*

"Ha, I knew he wouldn't catch me!" the crook said happily as she drove away. She was so busy celebrating, she didn't notice the flashing tracking device that was now attached to the roof of her car!

Duke continued his chase in the maze of sewer tunnels beneath the street, zipping through a smelly river of muck, slop, and sludge.

Duke grimaced. *"Pee-yew! I don't know what stinks more—the sewer, or the fact that Daisy got away."*

"According to my latest data," the police car said, "this is disgusting."

"You're right, as always," Duke replied.

"But with the transmitter and my maps of the tunnels under the city, we can cut her off," said the car.

"Great," said Duke, "we'll take her by surprise . . . if she doesn't smell us coming."

Meanwhile, Daisy calmly drove off, convinced she had made a perfect getaway. She thought she had gotten rid of Duke once and for all, but all of a sudden . . .

VROOOM!

Duke DeTain's car jumped out of a sewer hole and landed right in front of her!

"Stop! Police!" cried Duke.

He jumped out of his car, did a shoulder roll, and waved a pair of handcuffs at the crook.

Daisy slammed on her brakes.

She was so surprised by Duke's sudden appearance that she got out of the car and let him handcuff her without any fuss. "But what is that smell?" she said with a wince.

"That's the sweet smell of success," said the stinky police officer, "especially because you've racked up a quite a few charges today!"

Duke's car quickly printed three tickets.

"Bank robbery. Littering. Unauthorized use of explosives," Duke listed.

Suddenly, the police car printed one more ticket.

"Oh," said Duke, "and a bill for a deluxe car wash and police uniform dry cleaning!"

VOLCANO ADVENTURE

Based on the story by Margaret Wang

Base camp was buzzing with excitement! After months of planning for a volcano expedition, an explorer gathered his team together.

"We're going on a journey to the jewels, my friends," he said. "There are gemstones hidden in the volcanic rock at the top."

RUMBLE! RUMBLE! RUMBLE!

"Did you hear that?" a young miner asked, feeling nervous. "The volcano is waking up!"

"Actually, that was my stomach," the other miner admitted.

The scientist on the team reassured them. "I'll be monitoring the volcanic activity so we won't be

surprised by any sudden eruptions."

The explorer continued. "Here at base camp, the scientist and you, hungry miner, will be the brains and stomach of the operation. And you," he said to the other miner, "will come with me to the top of the volcano to collect samples."

He and the miner drove the exploration truck to the volcano's tip. The explorer put on his heat-resistant suit and stepped out onto the cooled lava.

"Excuse me, sir," the miner called from the

safety of the truck. "If the gems are in the lava, how will you know which rocks to collect?"

"I just know," the explorer said. Then his eyes fixed on a lump of volcanic rock. "This one looks perfect."

Back at base camp, a seismograph monitored the volcano. All was quiet. The scientist grinned and said, "Let's test the new drone."

The hungry miner flew the drone over base camp. The scientist was pleased. "This will help us map areas to look for the jewels," she said.

Then the hungry miner flew the drone over to the

lunch cart and landed it safely. *It'll also help me see what's for lunch,* he thought. *Mmm—sandwiches.*

Suddenly, the seismograph started making waves.

"Base to exploration truck," the scientist radioed. "We're seeing signs of possible tremors to come. You'd better get back, just in case."

The explorer and the young miner received the
message. The miner was disappointed.

"Can't we open that rock to see if there are any
gemstones inside?" he asked.

The explorer shook his head. "On my adventures,
I've learned that it's better to come back another
time than end up as lava slime," he rhymed.

They quickly loaded the huge rock onto the truck.
The crane groaned with the heavy weight.

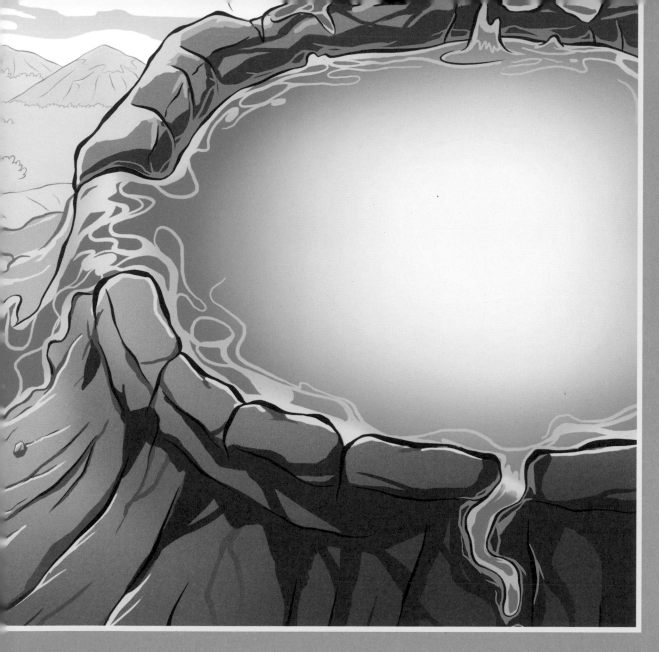

"Did you feel that?" the miner asked as the earth shook.

"Yes, my friend. But can you see that?" the explorer asked, nodding in the direction behind the miner.

In the distance, a thin trail of lava was slowly oozing out of the volcano.

"Don't worry," the explorer said. "This is normal for volcano expeditions. Let's check in with the brains of the operation."

The miner nodded and tried to relax.

"Exploration truck to base," the explorer radioed the scientist. "We have a situation."

"We can see from here," the scientist replied. The small trickle of lava was creeping closer. "The lava is moving slowly, but volcanic activity is increasing."

The lava was still far away, but it was good to get moving just in case. The young miner quickly started the truck's engine. *BRRRMMMM!*

"No need to rush, or we'll end up as lava mush," the explorer calmly rhymed. He released the hand brake so the miner could drive.

The truck made it back to base camp.

"How long until that lava stream gets here?" the explorer asked the scientist.

"You mean how long until the *two* lava streams get here," the scientist replied, studying the satellite feed. Another lava stream had formed on one side of the volcano and was heading toward the base.

"The lava is moving very slowly," the scientist reassured the team. "But we should end our exploring for today and come back when the activity has calmed down."

The explorer agreed. "We'll come back another day when the lava is at bay," he rhymed.

"How will we know if we're safe from the lava as we travel down the volcano?" the young miner asked.

"We can use the drone as our eye in the sky," said the scientist.

The scientist grabbed the drone and handed the remote control to the hungry miner. "It has heat protection, but the infrared camera will melt if you fly it too close to the lava."

"Drone lightly toasted, but not burnt. Got it," said the hungry miner, still thinking about food.

The hungry miner launched the drone. It scanned as it flew, displaying the area for the team on a monitor.

The team packed up the research base and prepared to leave in their various vehicles.

The explorer looked at the lava rock sample and said, "You've waited a long time to be discovered—you can wait a little more."

The team left base camp and headed off even farther away from the volcano. The scientist said, "The drone's monitor is showing a large rock formation ahead." She checked the lava flow. "The lava is still far away, but I don't think we can go over or around this wall of rock. We'll have to go through it!"

When they reached the rock formation, the explorer got into the excavator. The scientist watched the drone monitor and directed him as he began.

"This is basic science," she said. "A slow, steady force in one place will break the rock wall."

The explorer agreed. "It's okay to go slow if the drone's watching the lava flow!"

The excavator chipped away at the wall to open a path. The team was soon a safe distance away from the volcano.

"At least we know our new equipment works! The drone is awesome!" the scientist said. "When the volcano activity has calmed down, we can start again and collect more rocks."

"We do have one sample," he replied, his eyes lighting up with excitement.

The explorer unloaded the rock sample and got into the excavator again. The drill began whirring. After a few minutes, there was a gentle *CRACK*.

"Would you like to do the honors?" the explorer asked the young miner. The miner used his pickax to open the rock. Inside were shiny, precious gemstones!

"Aren't you going to say something wise that rhymes?" asked the miner.

The explorer thought for a moment and then mumbled quietly to himself, "This gemstone dream happened because we were a team? We took our time but made the volcano climb?"

The explorer marveled at the glimmering gems.

"Let's just say that good things come to those who wait," he said.

Just then, there was another rumble. It was the hungry miner's tummy again. "Well, I don't think I can wait for lunch much longer!" he said, and everyone laughed.

LEGO CITY

JUNGLE SECRETS

Based on the story by Steve Behling

"I'm bored!" said a glum voice.

"How can you be bored? We work at the Museum of Natural History! I love my job!" an archaeologist said as she spun a lasso while sitting near a dinosaur model.

"I love it, too!" said her bored fellow archaeologist. "But I'm ready for a real adventure. I want to get outside, find treasure . . . find excitement!"

"Excitement, eh? Then I have a mission for you!" said the museum director, bursting through the office door. She tossed a map across the room. The glum archaeologist snatched it eagerly.

"What is it?" he said, now excited.

"This old map belonged to an explorer who gave it to the museum," said the director. "Apparently, it leads to crystals hidden in the jungle. I need you to find those crystals, if they exist, and bring them back so we can display them in our museum."

Before she could say another word, the two archaeologists raced out of the museum and hopped on their vehicles.

VROOM!

"You can count on us!" they called.

"Be careful!" shouted the director. "The jungle is wild!"

But they couldn't hear her over the sound of their engines.

Hours later, the archaeologists arrived at the outskirts of the city. They entered the jungle, which was dense with trees, vines, bushes, and ferns. The brush was so thick! The adventurous archaeologist hopped off her motorcycle and used her machete to clear a path.

"Where are we?" she asked.

"We're close to the first marker," said her coworker.

"Then let's keep moving!" she replied.

"There it is!" yelled the other archaeologist. "The original explorer had to abandon the search for the crystals here."

"They sure didn't make it very far," she said. "Let's see if we can do better!"

"Wait!" said her coworker, grabbing her by the arm. "I can see a statue behind those trees. I think it holds a crystal!"

"Sundew!" he suddenly hollered in a frightened
voice. "Giant sundew!"

Just then, the giant sundew snapped its jawlike
leaves. It was blocking their way to the crystal!

"Don't move!" said the adventurous archaeologist.
"I'll handle this."

"Do you have a plan?" asked her coworker. "I've
never seen such a big sundew before!"

"I'll use my lasso!" she said. "I hope all that
practice at the museum wasn't for nothing."

The coworker stood still as she spun the lasso
above her head and then threw it gently, winding it
around the sundew's jawlike leaves. Then she tied
it into a bow.

"Aww, what a pretty plant!" said the other
archaeologist.

The adventurous archaeologist approached the statue and picked up the crystal.

"We've got the first one!" she said joyfully.

As they rushed off with the crystal, they saw that the cunning sundew was already untying the bow in its leaves.

"Fortunately, sundews can't run," said the adventurous archaeologist. "They also make fascinating houseplants . . . if they are regular size, of course!"

"But s-s-snakes can run, r-r-right?" her friend
stammered. Staring them in the face was a very large,
very hungry SNAKE! It was twisted around the
second stone statue . . . with another of the crystals!

This time, the adventurous archaeologist didn't
know what to do—she'd always been scared of
snakes! But her companion had an idea.

He dug into his backpack, took out a weird-looking

flute, and started to play a monotonous tune.

"I knew those recorder lessons would come in handy one day!" he said. The snake started writhing in a dance, with a hypnotized expression on its scaled face. "Now we can grab the crystal!"

"Whew, another close call!" said the adventurous archaeologist, gently removing the crystal from the statue.

Without warning, a leopard darted from the jungle and grabbed the map from them!

"Hey! You! No stealing!" one archaeologist yelled loudly. They jumped into their jeep. "Follow that leopard!" *ZOOM!*

They chased the leopard in the jeep. They couldn't lose that map! The jungle terrain was rough, and the

jeep bounced everywhere. The leopard ran and ran.

"How fast can that thing go?" asked the adventurous archaeologist.

"Leopards have a top speed of about thirty-seven miles per hour," answered her coworker.

"Oh, no," she said. "On this ground, it can outrun us easily!"

The leopard raced over a low, rickety bridge, and they followed.

"There he is!" shouted one of them, pointing.

"And there he goes!" his coworker replied as the leopard jumped off the bridge and into the river below. "Grab the kayaks from the jeep and hit the water!"

SPLASH!

The chase was on—again!

The river raged as the archaeologists caught up to the leopard!

Suddenly, the leopard leaped to a nearby tree. The map fell from its mouth—and into one of their laps!

"What luck!" he exclaimed.

"You can say that, but . . . this is a waterfall!" she shouted. They paddled and paddled, but the current was too strong. They were going to go over the waterfall!

"Need a lift?"

The archaeologists heard a voice over a loudspeaker and looked up. It was the museum director in a helicopter! "Grab the cable!" she called. "I'll pull you up!"

Phew! The helicopter rescued the pair, and they landed at the bottom of the waterfall. They spied a cavern hidden behind it.

"That's the last location, according to the map!" said one of the archaeologists. They entered the cavern and found the remaining statues . . . and the crystals!

"Eureka!" cried the museum director. "You've done it! You two aren't just archaeologists . . . you're real jungle explorers!"

The archaeologists gently placed the crystals in their backpacks.

"The crystals will have a good home in the Museum of Natural History, where everyone will get to see them," said the museum director. "I am curious about one thing, though. How did you get the other crystals?"

"Well," said the adventurous jungle explorer, "our hobbies finally came in handy!"

THE FIRE SPIRIT

**Based on a story from the Fire Department archives
by Maciej Andrysiak**

At the city's fire station, the firefighters sat in front of the TV, watching a report on the space shuttle landing. Unfortunately, the shuttle had recently disappeared from the radar, and no one knew where the astronaut was.

To lighten the worried mood, Fire Chief Chandler told the tale of his encounter with the legendary Fire Spirit.

"It all began one quiet morning in the forest," he said. "The green valley was half blanketed in darkness.

"Then a powerful blast whistled over the dense forest. There was a puff and a crash, and the valley fell silent. It looked like a storm, but there was no thunder.

"Suddenly, a white figure loomed amid the flames. The figure stepped slowly and calmly, as if it wasn't afraid of anything!"

"And it was the Fire Spirit?" asked Horace.

"And how!" replied Fire Chief Chandler. "When it looked at me, it sent shivers down my spine! And when it left, the place where it had stood was scorched to ashes!"

"Wow!" said Horace.

"Incredible!" said Bart.

"I'd sure like to meet it someday!" Horace said.

From the next room, the cook called everyone to breakfast. The door flew open, and a firefighter in a fur-lined flight jacket burst into the station. She took off her cap and tossed it across the room—where it landed right on the hat rack— and strode toward the table.

"Well, well, look who's here!" The fire chief smiled. "It's Sam, our irreplaceable pilot!"

"She can always sniff out breakfast!" another firefighter shouted.

"The eye of a hawk and a keen sense of smell," Sam admitted as she sat down at the table. "That's me!"

"And a hearty appetite," said one of the firefighters as everyone chuckled.

Horace stared at the pilot for a moment, then whispered to Bart, "I'd like to have a cap like that someday and be the pilot of a fire plane."

With her keen ear, the pilot caught the remark.

"You don't need a cap yet," she said. "For now, you should practice with a fire extinguisher!"

Horace reddened as the other firefighters laughed. But before he could give it another thought, the siren wailed.

"Fire! Fire!" the chief cried, leaping from his seat. "Prepare the equipment and the fire engines!"

Bart and Horace slid down the fire pole. The mighty ladder trucks were already pulling out of the garage. The firefighters jumped in, and they were off.

Horace gulped. "Aw, I didn't even touch my breakfast."

The sky over the forest was black with smoke from the burning trees. A mysterious white figure stepped slowly among the forest as the flames approached from all sides. It walked as if it didn't even notice the fire.

Suddenly, it stopped. It seemed to hear the sirens from the approaching fire engines. The figure turned and, with a steady stride, headed toward the new sound.

Horace and Bart looked at the wooded hills. A yellow flame shot straight up over the trees. The firefighters had already started up the water pumps and were preparing the hoses.

"Catch!" Horace said, tossing his friend a fire extinguisher.

The smoke covered everything around them, and it was very hot. But protected by their fire suits, the firefighters bravely entered the flames.

"It's Sam!" cried Bart, pointing to the sky. "Soon she'll release the water!"

"Hey! You need to help the guys in the valley," Fire Chief Chandler said. "But be careful—there's smoke everywhere and you can't see a thing. It's hard to get there." He stopped and looked around. "The best bet would be from the air!"

Horace's face lit up with a smile as he recalled the words of the pilot: "For now, you should practice with a fire extinguisher!"

"I think I have an idea!" he cried joyfully.

Horace grabbed the fire extinguisher and mounted it like a steed. With one quick move, he released the valve with the foam, and the fire extinguisher shot through the air like a missile— with Horace aboard! The brave firefighter flew on the foam-shooting extinguisher. As he zipped above the forest, the foam splashed all around, putting out the flames.

He spun a few more loops as the fire died out in the clearing. But soon the extinguisher spat out the last of its foam and Horace began to fall!

Horace deftly avoided the trees and bushes, but he struck a stump with the fire extinguisher and landed face-first in the dirt. *Apparently, I haven't mastered landing yet,* he thought.

He was sticking out of the ground, thrashing his legs, when someone tugged him loose. Once he was free, he brushed off the dirt and leaves and saw a mysterious white figure looming over him, charred from smoke and flames. The sight frightened him.

"Help! Help!" he cried. "The Fire Spirit!"

The white figure
reached out a hand and
touched the firefighter
on the shoulder.

"Are you all right?"
Horace heard the
figure say.

"No! No!" he cried,
clamping his eyes shut.
"Don't eat me!"

The figure stopped.
"What? I was thinking
about calling for a
doctor."

Just then, something
whistled from behind
Horace and flashed
over his head. The
white figure quickly
ducked to avoid Bart,
who was screaming as
he whizzed by on a fire
extinguisher.

"Leave my friend
alone, you creature!"
Bart shouted. He
threatened the figure
with his fist.

Unfortunately, he forgot to steer the fire extinguisher, and just as he made his most dangerous-looking face, his flight ended when he crashed into a tree.

As the smoke cleared, shapes began to return to normal and everything was visible again. The white figure lifted its arms to a huge helmet and removed it. A pleasant but somewhat stunned face emerged. The figure gazed at the firefighter dangling in the branches, covered with white foam that was gushing from the nearby fire extinguisher.

"And I thought after the space flight, nothing would surprise me anymore," the figure said.

Horace jumped for joy.

"You're the lost astronaut!" he shouted.

"I didn't get lost," she explained, looking around the forest. "I had a fuel leak and had to make an emergency landing. I got into a little trouble here. The fuel caught fire when I landed!"

Back at the fire station, everything was quiet again. Horace was watching the astronaut on TV. He was describing his entire adventure—from his emergency landing to his encounter with the firefighters.

Suddenly, the door burst open, and Sam strutted into the station. She took off her cap and tossed it across the room. It landed on the table in front of Horace.

Horace was surprised to see the pilot, but Sam smiled. "No one has ever started out by flying on a fire extinguisher! But this must be a sign that he'll be a great pilot! The cap is yours. Starting tomorrow, I'm going to give you flying lessons!"

Horace stood and shyly tried on the cap. When he looked in the mirror, he saw that it fit him perfectly.

A WILD LIFE

Based on the story by Joshua Pruett

Westbrook W. Sleet was the host of the TV show *Wild Wilderness.* He and his camera operator, Toby, were working on a new episode.

"Today we're in the jungle, near an animal rescue camp!" said Westbrook into a microphone. "The jungle is full of endangered species!"

"Wh-wh-what if that endangered species is us?" Toby said, spotting a lioness behind them. "Um . . . should we run?"

"YES!" Westbrook yelled. "But keep filming!"

They ran toward the animal rescue camp. And so did the lioness!

When they reached the camp, the lioness stopped.

"Don't worry about Mina," a woman there said calmly. She gave the big cat a piece of meat. "She wasn't chasing you. She was just running home for her afternoon snack. I'm Lydia Lighthouse, chief veterinarian. We're so glad to have you both here. We love your show! Let me give you a tour of the camp."

Lydia's team looked after lots of wild animals, including Mina. The camp also had all kinds of special equipment and vehicles. Lydia introduced Westbrook

and Toby to the rest of her team. There was Mikko the veterinarian, helicopter pilot Carla, and fearless driver Perry.

Just then, a monkey came over and hugged Westbrook.

"Meet Ivy," said Lydia. "She was injured and we nursed her back to health. Now she's all better—but she's also a real prankster!"

A moment later, Ivy stole Westbrook's microphone!

Lydia couldn't help laughing. Westbrook and Toby watched helplessly as the cheeky monkey ran away!

"*Oooh! Oooh!*" said the monkey.

But before Westbrook could catch Ivy, an alarm sounded. It was an animal emergency! Suddenly, everyone was on the move. The crew jumped into action. There wasn't a single second to lose!

The entire animal rescue team headed out.
Carla led the way in her helicopter, while Perry
followed them in his all-terrain vehicle.
     As they got close to the river, the team heard
a baby animal crying for help.
     "That sound is coming from the riverbed,"
said Lydia.

"We can't see what kind of trouble this animal is in," Lydia explained. "But this will give us a bird's-eye view." She handed Westbrook and Toby a large drone.

Westbrook took the controller and Toby launched the drone into the air. A small monitor on the controller showed them everything the drone was recording as it flew above.

When the drone approached the riverbed, Westbrook spotted something on the monitor.

"There's a lion cub trapped between the rocks!" he yelled. "And a tree is blocking its way out!"

Lydia started thinking of a plan. Then Westbrook noticed something else on the monitor. Something moving.

"Wait, there's a big log floating toward him," Westbrook said.

Lydia took the controller from him and looked at the screen.

"That's not a log!" Lydia cried. "That's a croc! We need to rescue that lion cub RIGHT NOW!"

Everyone sprang into action and began working together to help the cub.

Carla used her helicopter to carry away the fallen tree. Then Perry used his all-terrain vehicle to clear the rocks out of the way.

Toby and Lydia distracted the crocodile with meat snacks. But Westbrook had the most important job. He slid down into the riverbed to rescue the lion cub.

Thankfully, the cub ran right to him! Everyone cheered. The lion cub was saved!

Westbrook held the sleeping cub on his lap all the way back to camp.

"I wanted to film the rescue," Toby said sadly, "but when I went to grab my camera from the jeep, all I found was this banana peel!"

Westbrook squinted at the banana peel. "A banana stole your camera?"

Lydia burst out laughing, and then Toby understood.

"What a cheeky monkey!" he grumbled. Ivy had taken his camera!

When the team returned to the animal rescue camp, Ivy was waiting. She'd had the camera the whole time. She had even somehow pressed the Record button! Toby looked at the footage—the monkey had recorded the entire rescue! Westbrook and Toby were thrilled.

Before they left, Westbrook filmed one last shot of the camp. Suddenly, there was a loud *ROAR!*

It was Mina the lioness! She was staring at Toby's camera and didn't seem happy.

"I g-g-guess Mina doesn't like being f-f-filmed," said Toby, shaking with fear. "Should we run?"

"YES!" Westbrook yelled. He quickly ran away and accidentally dropped the camera.

Mina chased Toby and Westbrook back into the jungle.

The monkey hit Record on the camera.

"Keep it rolling, Ivy," cried Westbrook. "This is the really exciting part!"

Ivy agreed: *"Oooh! Oooh!"*